This igloo book belongs to:

_____

igloobooks

Published in 2021
First published in the UK by Igloo Books Ltd
An imprint of Igloo Books Ltd
Cottage Farm, NN6 0BJ, UK
Owned by Bonnier Books
Sveavägen 56, Stockholm, Sweden
www.igloobooks.com

0221 001
2 4 6 8 10 9 7 5 3 1
ISBN 978-1-80022-648-7

Printed and manufactured in China

FAIRY
Magic

igloobooks

One day, Annie spent ages at the bottom of her garden.
"What are you doing?" asked Mummy.
"I'm looking for fairies," replied Annie, "but there aren't any."

"Come on," said Mummy, "let's go back inside and I'll get you a nice drink."

Inside, Annie sat at the kitchen table and had a drink of orange juice. "Maybe fairies don't exist," she said, sadly, looking up at Mummy.

"Of course they do," said Mummy, giving Annie a lovely cuddle, "but they are very shy. Maybe you could write them a letter."

So, Annie wrote a special letter to the fairies.

Dear Fairies,

Mummy says you live at the bottom of our garden. I looked for you, but couldn't see you anywhere.

If you are real, please would you come and see me?

Love,

Annie xxx

The next morning, to Annie's amazement, she found a letter on her pillow.

The Fairies
The Bottom of
the Garden

Dear Annie,

Thank you for your letter.
Your mummy is right, we do
live at the bottom of your garden
and we are very shy. We hope to see
you soon. Keep writing!

Love,

The Fairies

xxx

Annie was puzzled by the letter. The writing looked a bit like Mummy's. "I wonder if Mummy wrote the letter and not the fairies?" she thought.

Annie wasn't sure that she even believed in fairies. She had gone to all the trouble of writing to them, but they hadn't come to see her.

That night, when Annie went to sleep, she had a strange dream. She dreamt that she was a fairy and the little fairies in her garden had invited her to their picnic. There were cupcakes and flower drinks and fairy games.

When Annie woke up, she decided to write another letter to the fairies. "Maybe they are real after all," she thought.

The Fairies
The Bottom of
the Garden
26 Thistle Lane

Dear Fairies,

Thank you for your letter. Last night, I had a dream about you.

I would really love to see if you look the same as in my dream. Please, please, come and visit me.

Love,

Annie xxx

The next morning, Annie came downstairs and
found a postcard on the doormat, addressed to her.
On top of it was a cupcake that looked delicious.

Annie felt very excited as she settled down to read what the fairies had written.

Annie
26 Thistle Lane

Dear Annie,

It was very nice to hear from you again.
How lovely that you had a dream about us!
Here is a little gift for you. It is one of our extra-special, fairy cupcakes.
Enjoy eating it!
Love from, The Fairies xxx

When Annie had finished reading the postcard, she sat down and looked at the fairy cupcake. She smiled as she thought how much like one of Mummy's cupcakes it looked. "I bet it was really Mummy who made this cake and wrote the letter, she said," taking a big bite.

The cupcake was yummy, it tasted of toffee caramel and vanilla cream. Even though it really did taste like one of Mummy's cakes, Annie couldn't help noticing that the cupcake sparkled and tasted extra-delicious.

Annie made sure that Mummy saw her taking the letter into the garden. "Make sure you leave it in the fairy ring," called Mummy. "Then the fairies will know it is extra-special."

Among the flowers was a little ring of red and white toadstools. Annie stepped carefully into the middle and gently laid her letter down on the grass.

She closed her eyes and made a special wish:
"Fairies, fairies, come to me.
If you are real, then let me see."

Just as Annie opened her eyes, she was sure she saw little shapes flitting in amongst the flowers.

"I must be imagining things," she thought, "but I hope the fairies send me a reply to my letter soon."

The next day, Annie found a wonderful surprise on
her pillow. It was an invitation to a party from the fairies!

We, The Fairies,
would like to invite
you, our special friend, to a
picnic at 12.30pm at the bottom of
the garden.

With love,
The Fairies xxxxx

At first, Annie felt very excited. Then, she felt worried. What if it *was* Mummy who was secretly writing the letters? What if Annie got all dressed up and the fairies didn't come? If they didn't exist, she would be very disappointed.

Annie ran upstairs and flung open her wardrobe. She pulled out her floaty fairy dress and her special pair of fairy wings. She even found a fairy wand in her toy box.

Annie brushed her hair and put her prettiest hair slide in. She put on her bracelets, her flower necklace and her pretty pink party pumps. "I'm ready," thought Annie and she went downstairs and out into the garden.

Annie crept past the kitchen window, where Mummy
was busy washing up. She was sure she could hear tinkling
laughter coming from the bottom of the garden.